How do make pancakes?

Contents

Written by Barbara MacKay

Illustrated by Szilvia Szakall

Collins

What's in this book?

Listen and say

chocolate

pancakes

sugar

lemon

Download the audio at www.collins.co.uk/839644

Let's make pancakes

Pete is reading his new book.

"What's in your book, Pete," asks Mum.

"Lots of nice food," says Pete. "I'm hungry. Ooh, pancakes! Can we make pancakes?"

4

"I don't know," says Mum. "Let's see. What do we need?"

"There's a list," says Pete. "Have we got these things?"

You need ...

You need a pan, a bowl and a big spoon.
Put everything on the table.

Now, wash your hands. You need to be clean.

Now you need some flour, some milk and some eggs.

Look and read. How much flour do you need?

2 cups of flour
4 cups of milk
2 eggs

How much milk do you need?
How many eggs do you need?

Step 1

Put the flour in the bowl. You need two cups. Be careful!

Step 2

Now, add four cups of milk to the bowl.

Now, use the spoon. Stir the flour and milk.

Be careful!

Step 3

Open the eggs. One … two ….
Don't drop the eggs on
the table!

Hold the spoon. Stir the eggs, the milk and
the flour.

Step 4

You need a pan. Put some oil in the pan.
Ask Mum to help!

Be careful! It's very hot.

Put the pancake mixture into the hot pan.
Cook the pancake. Then ... flip!

It isn't easy to flip a pancake. Ask Mum to help.

If it's difficult ... try again!

Now, you can flip your pancakes.
Well, done!

How many pancakes do you want
to make? You can make a lot of pancakes
and put them on a plate.

Step 5

What do you want on your pancake?
You can add lemon, sugar ... or chocolate!

"I want some chocolate!" says Pete.

Making pancakes is fun and it's easy!
Do you want to make some
pancakes, too?

Picture dictionary

Listen and repeat

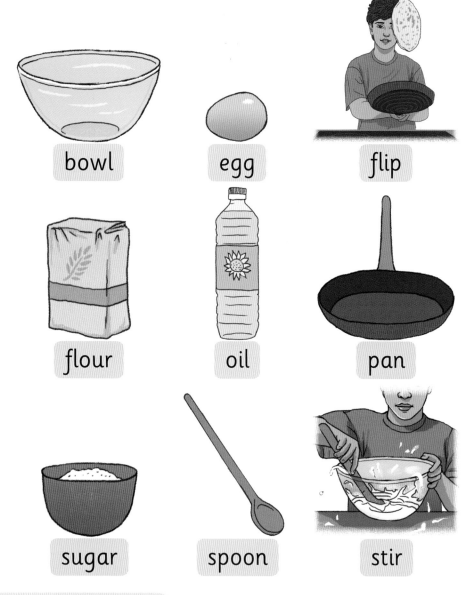

bowl

egg

flip

flour

oil

pan

sugar

spoon

stir

1 Look and order

2 Listen and say

Collins

Published by Collins
An imprint of HarperCollins*Publishers*
Westerhill Road
Bishopbriggs
Glasgow
G64 2QT

HarperCollins*Publishers*
1st Floor, Watermarque Building
Ringsend Road
Dublin 4
Ireland

William Collins' dream of knowledge for all began with the publication of his first book in 1819.

A self-educated mill worker, he not only enriched millions of lives, but also founded a flourishing publishing house. Today, staying true to this spirit, Collins books are packed with inspiration, innovation and practical expertise. They place you at the centre of a world of possibility and give you exactly what you need to explore it.

© HarperCollins*Publishers* Limited 2020

10 9 8 7 6 5 4 3 2

ISBN 978-0-00-839644-2

www.collins.co.uk/elt

British Library Cataloguing in Publication Data

A catalogue record for this publication is available from the British Library.

Author: Barbara MacKay
Illustrator: Szilvia Szakall (Beehive)
Series editor: Rebecca Adlard
Commissioning editor: Zoë Clarke
Publishing manager: Lisa Todd
Product managers: Jennifer Hall and Caroline Green
In-house editor: Alma Puts Keren
Project manager: Emily Hooton
Editor: Frances Amrani
Proofreaders: Natalie Murray and Michael Lamb
Cover designer: Kevin Robbins
Typesetter: 2Hoots Publishing Services Ltd
Audio produced by id audio, London
Reading guide author: Emma Wilkinson
Production controller: Rachel Weaver
Printed and bound by: GPS Group, Slovenia

Download the audio for this book and a reading guide for parents and teachers at www.collins.co.uk/839644